I0829668

LUST
IS
MY FAVORITE
SIN

The Dirty Archangel`s journey
into the Dark Side

3 Demons

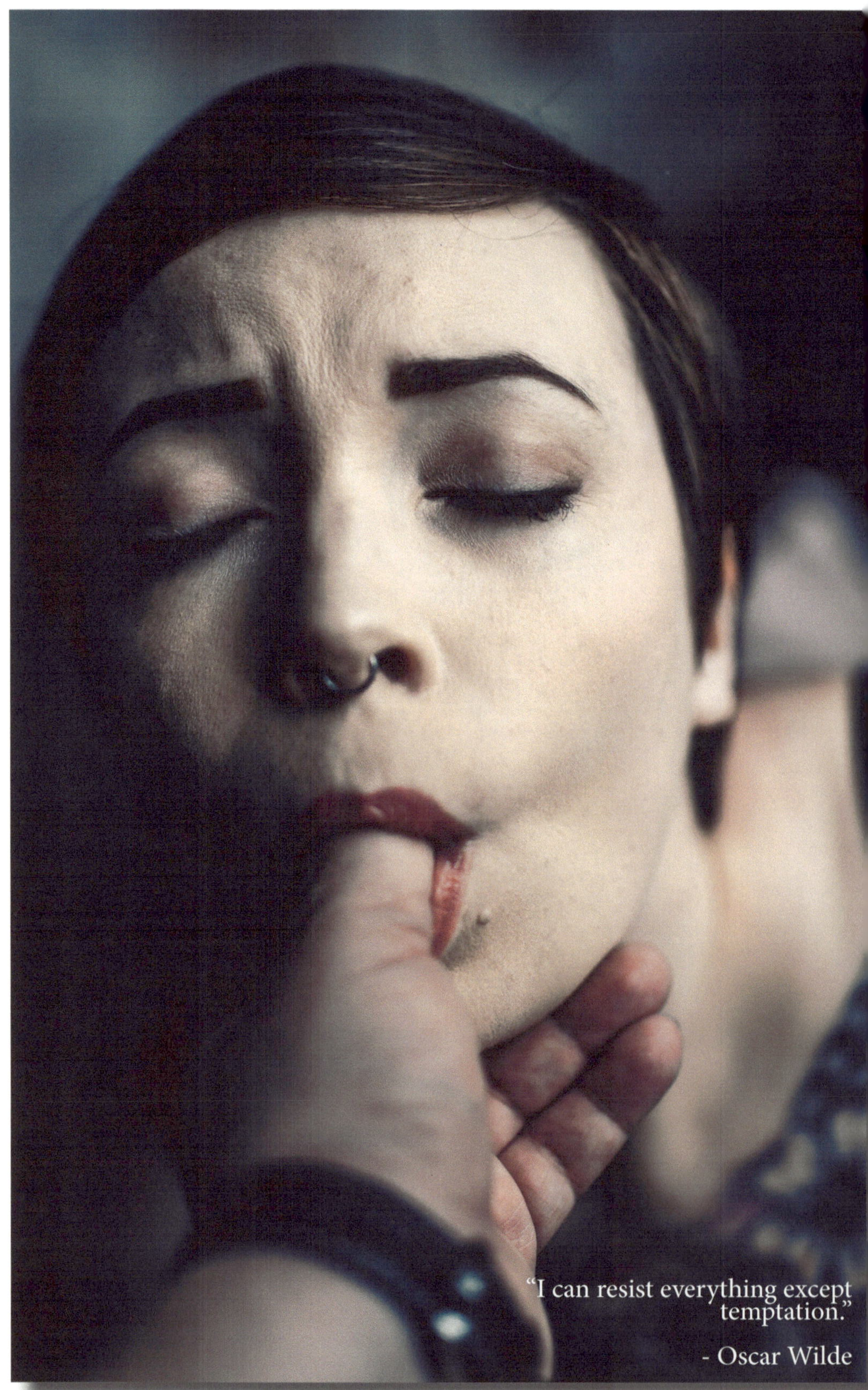
"I can resist everything except temptation."
- Oscar Wilde

What is BDSM?

Bondage & Discipline - Domination & Submission - Sadism & Masochism

As a hedonist and philocalist, I came to believe that pleasure is the main drive behind every action we perform, behind every life decisions we make. Sex is just one of the countless ways that we can access pleasure in the most direct way. Although the act of having sex is a natural, crucial part of our biological existence, our society made it very complicated. Society forbade so many things they did not understand. Things became taboo, taboos became fetishes which is a form of sexual desire in which gratification is linked to an abnormal degree to a particular object, item or a part of the body. And society forced us to stop talking about taboos, fetishes, sex. We humiliated people who seek pleasure through taboo concepts and fetishized things. BDSM is just one of the wide variety of concepts our society turned into taboo.

BDSM, in its truest form, is a power exchange between Dominant/Dom (male or female) and Submissive/Sub (male or female). I`d like to put emphasis on the word "exchange". Contrary to popular belief, BDSM is not about Dominant party doing whatever they want to do to Submissive party. It is a two-way mind game, sexual interaction between Dom and Sub that involves satisfaction at a different level than normal sex. In a true BDSM relationship, there is no abuse, there is no mistreatment, there is no fooling your partner. Submissive defines all the rules and Dominant`s first and most important responsibility is to respect those rules. After rules are defined, Dominant can dominate his/her Sub however they want inside those boundaries. A Dom cannot do anything to a Sub that he or she clearly specified that Dom could do. This is why communication is one of the most important, most fundamental parts of a BDSM relationship. Every detail, every act is communicated so no harm comes to Sub. Another most important factor in a BDSM relationship is safety. People who practice BDSM relationships are the people who like to push boundaries. Both mental and physical limits are tested and pushed. This is the reason safety is always the most important factor in a BDSM play. Safety is achieved through communication and respect. Safeword must be defined and when a Sub uses safeword during a sexual play, everything stops without hesitation, without question.

As a Dominant man, an artist and a poet; I wanted to give you a chance to look into a Dominant man`s mind, his desires, his cravings and his approach to his Submissive woman with total respect for who she is.
I hope you will enjoy and love it

Dirty Archangel

You are entering where there is no mercy.
Proceed with caution
knowing
your screams, your begging
will bring you no escape.

7 Demons

I am
the dirty Archangel
the demons bow to.
I bath in sin.
I feast on lust.
I carry the mark of Sodom
embedded in my heart.
I take my breakfast
in the dungeons of
Dante`s circle of lust.
I travel to Hell
for dinner with Lucifer.
Pleasure is my drug and
lust is my favorite sin.

9 Demons

I don't make love
to my woman,
loving is weak.
I hurt my woman.
I kiss so hard
her lips hurt.
I slam against the wall
her back hurts.
I thrust so hard
her thighs hurt.
Her hair, her throat.
When I'm done with her,
her very soul hurts,
begging me to hurt her more.

11 Demons

When I thrust into
your pussy so deep,
your halo will burst
into blazing flames.
I will grab your wings
and make you cum so loud,
every Angel up in heaven
will cross their legs
hearing your screams.
They will get in line
to come down to my dungeon.

13 Demons

Fight me, babygirl.
Let me show you
how good you will look
slammed against the wall,
thrown onto bed
and choked from behind.
Let me show you
how amazing you will sound
with every hit
of my belt on your ass.
You are strong,
fight me, I like it.
Just remember,
I am stronger.

15 Demons

I don`t care about your clothes.
I want to undress your mind,
get your soul naked
in front of my desires.
I don`t care about
opening your legs wide.
I want to see you parting
your inhibitions first
and destroying them all.
I don`t care about
who you were before you met me.
I will set you free,
destroy the cage you've been stuck in
and help you become
who you were meant to be.

17 Demons

What turns me on is not
what I do to your body,
it is what I do to your mind.

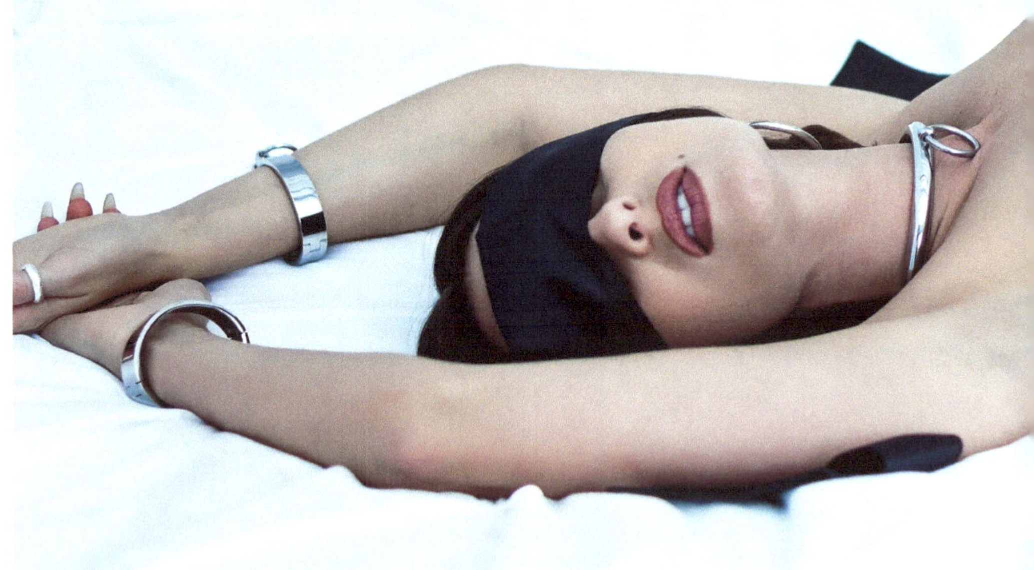

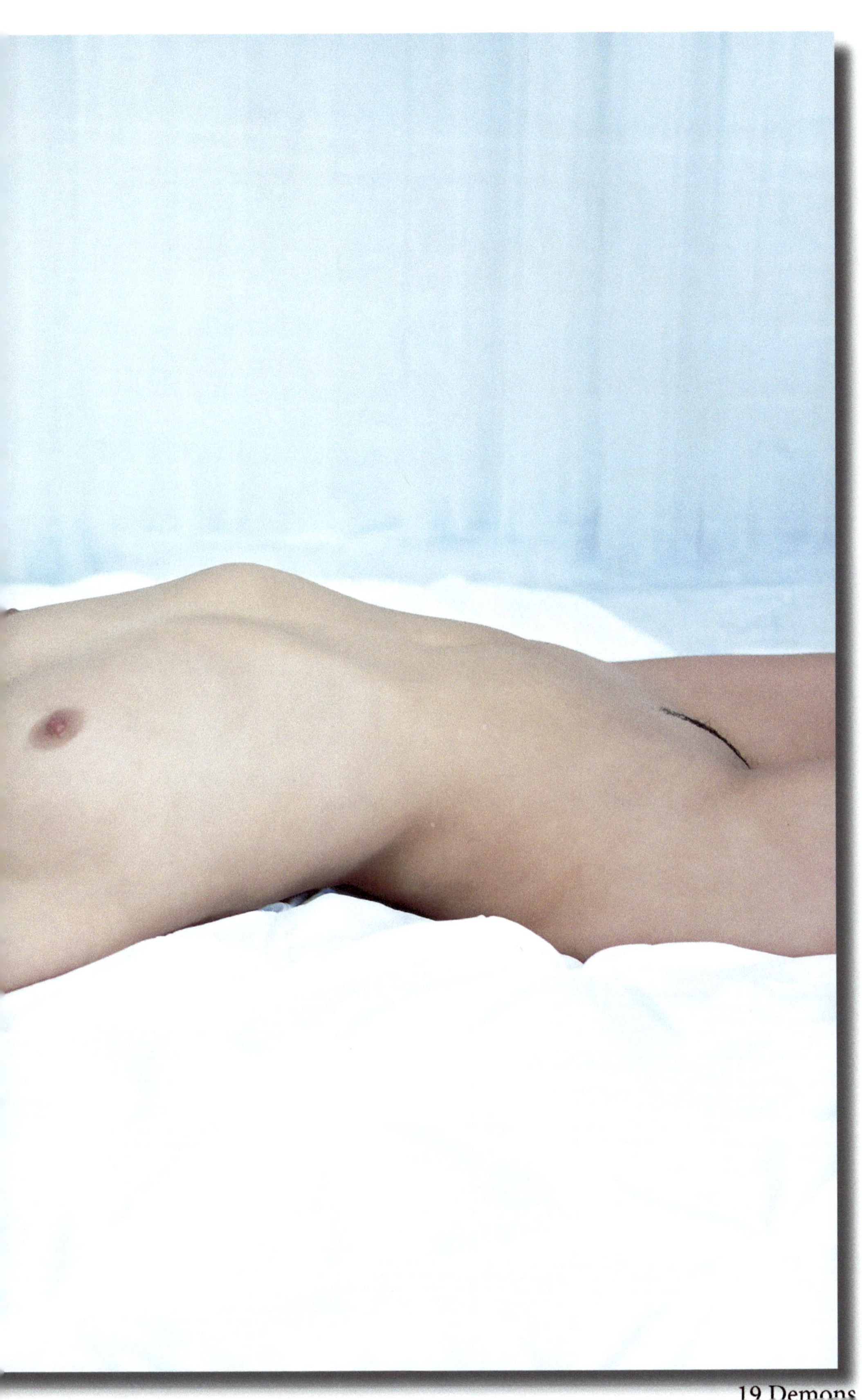

19 Demons

I am looking at all these pathetic people.
They are eating without tasting,
talking without meaning,
consuming without satisfying,
owning without earning and
fucking without feeling.
Without feeling the earthquakes
that shake their foundation.
They are just existing
without living.

21 Demons

Look into my eyes, babygirl.
You are my little whore
and you will do as you are told.
Everything you are belongs to me.
I will redefine every word for you.
You will find out what
rough really means.
You will learn how it feels
when you are owned by a real man.
Your whole world will shatter
when you see how a woman
gets truly dominated.

Nothing tastes better
than a good girl's lips
covered with my warm cum
after I have pulled out my cock,
when her wide open eyes
are begging me for air
while choking and gagging.

25 Demons

I want the craving
that will end
all the other cravings.
I want the kiss
to forget
the hottest kiss before.
I desire
for the explosion
that will make me growl
like I never have before.
I want to read the book
that will make all the books
I have read before
meaningless.
I want to read the book
that will make all the books
I have read before
meaningful.

27 Demons

When the world was at war,
we kept fucking.
When the world came to an end,
we kept fucking.
The world you and I knew
had already ended
when your skin touched my skin.
We didn't care about anything
after that moment.

29 Demons

Let me
show you
the difference
between
a blowjob and
a mouthfuck.

Behind
the shadows,
we buried
each other's demons
deep under our skin.
We didn't realize
each demon we killed,
brought us closer
to the point of
no return.
We both knew
we didn't give a fuck
when our lips
touched each other
for the first time,
that was our point of no return.

33 Demons

I put a chain on you
because you are mine.

I will take down churches
with your screams.
Your moaning will vibrate the foundation
as I thrust myself into you at the altar.
The crucifix will burn in flames
while I drink the wine between your legs.
I will push harder and harder behind you
under Qubba, as I kiss your arched back.
My demons and I will fill all your holes
on the stairs of Mihrab.
We will bathe in the tub of our sins.
We will get drunk with every wave of pleasure
and laugh at the morons who are waiting
for their Angels to take them
up to their heaven.
They do not know that I left
their Angels breathless,
at the doorstep of a synagogue,
where I fucked their brains out.

She has never experienced
something so primitively strong,
nobody in her life has challenged her
and came out on top.
Yet, the look in his eyes invaded
every second and every moment.
His gaze made her knees weak.
The desire to get down on her knees,
undeniably, became her only wish.
His grip on her throat and
his orders in her ears became
the only things that fed her cravings.
The constant wetness between her legs
seems to be getting worse with
the thought of his growl in her mind.
Finally, she knows what it feels like
to be a real woman.
Finally, she knows what it feels like
to be owned.

39 Demons

The real chains
that bind you to me
are not the ones I put
on your wrists and ankles.
It is the way I own your soul
and your mind.
Your addiction to my words
that brings out your darkest fantasies.
The poison I inject into your mind
that makes you let me do anything
I want to do to your body.
Those are the real chains I forge,
deep down in my dungeons.

You wanted a barbarous fuck?
Hold on to my horns, babygirl.
Your master, the King of Hell
Lord of Demons, will take you
on a ride, you have never had before.
I will stretch every hole,
in your not so fragile body,
to limits you didn't know you had.
Our blazing flames will reach
all the way up to heaven
and burn those fucking tiny wings.
I will go so deep as I growl
between your legs, as I burn
deeper than the deepest dungeon
that we locked our darkest desires in.
Galaxies will be collapsing,
stars will be destroyed,
while you scream my name
to both heaven and hell.

"Do your toes,
those little fingers
on your beautiful feet,
do they ever sing?"
I asked her.
She looked puzzled,
not understanding
what I tried to ask,
and said "No."
I grabbed her throat,
threw her onto the bed,
grabbed her ankles and
pushed her legs up
next to her head.
Her amazing, soaked pussy
exposed and opened
like a fully bloomed rose.
I attacked her pussy
with my lips and my tongue.
Her screams mixed with
the music that her curled toes
played by hitting invisible keys
on the invisible piano.
Her toes composed and sang
the most beautiful piece
I have ever heard with my conducting.

He poured wine over her pussy,
drinking the wine between her lips
as his tongue moved up and down.
He was getting drunk from the wine,
while she was getting drunk
from the tongue that was doing
the most exotic dance with her clit.

Yes, I am a gentleman.
The kind of gentleman
who will not let you breathe
while choking on my thick meat,
until I see the tears
streaming down your cheeks.
The kind of gentleman who will
show no mercy to your throat
and choke you until you see stars,
while cumming all over,
convulsing and screaming.
The kind of gentleman who will
hold you in my arms,
kissyour hair softly and caress you.

My little fucktoy,
My cumslut,
My dirty little whore,
My pet,
My sweet babygirl,
My slave,
My property…
These are the sweet words I like
whispering into your ears
as my morning cock spasms
inside your exploding pussy.
You will carry my cum inside you
all day long and remember,
when each drop streams down your panties,
that you are owned and loved.

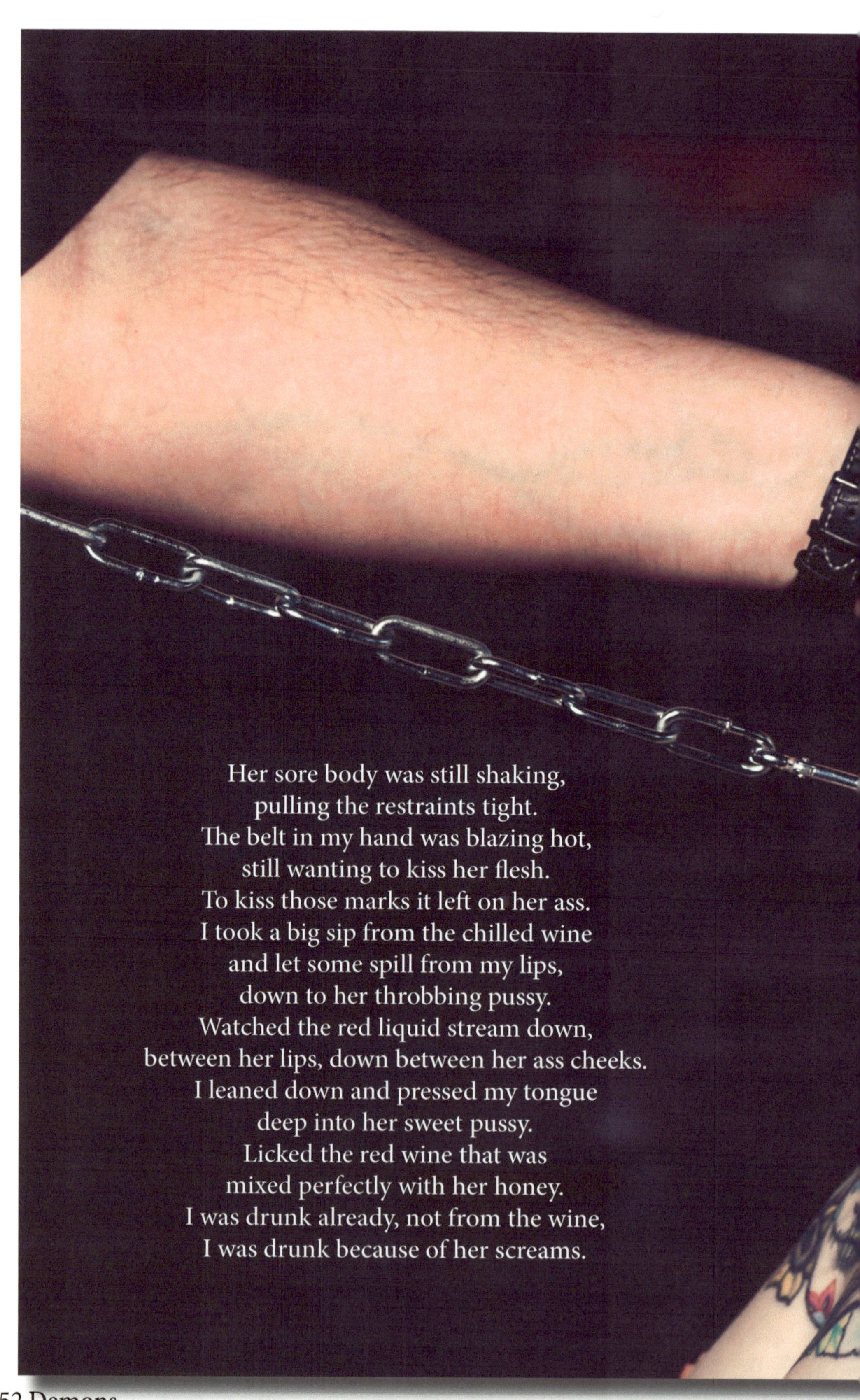

Her sore body was still shaking,
pulling the restraints tight.
The belt in my hand was blazing hot,
still wanting to kiss her flesh.
To kiss those marks it left on her ass.
I took a big sip from the chilled wine
and let some spill from my lips,
down to her throbbing pussy.
Watched the red liquid stream down,
between her lips, down between her ass cheeks.
I leaned down and pressed my tongue
deep into her sweet pussy.
Licked the red wine that was
mixed perfectly with her honey.
I was drunk already, not from the wine,
I was drunk because of her screams.

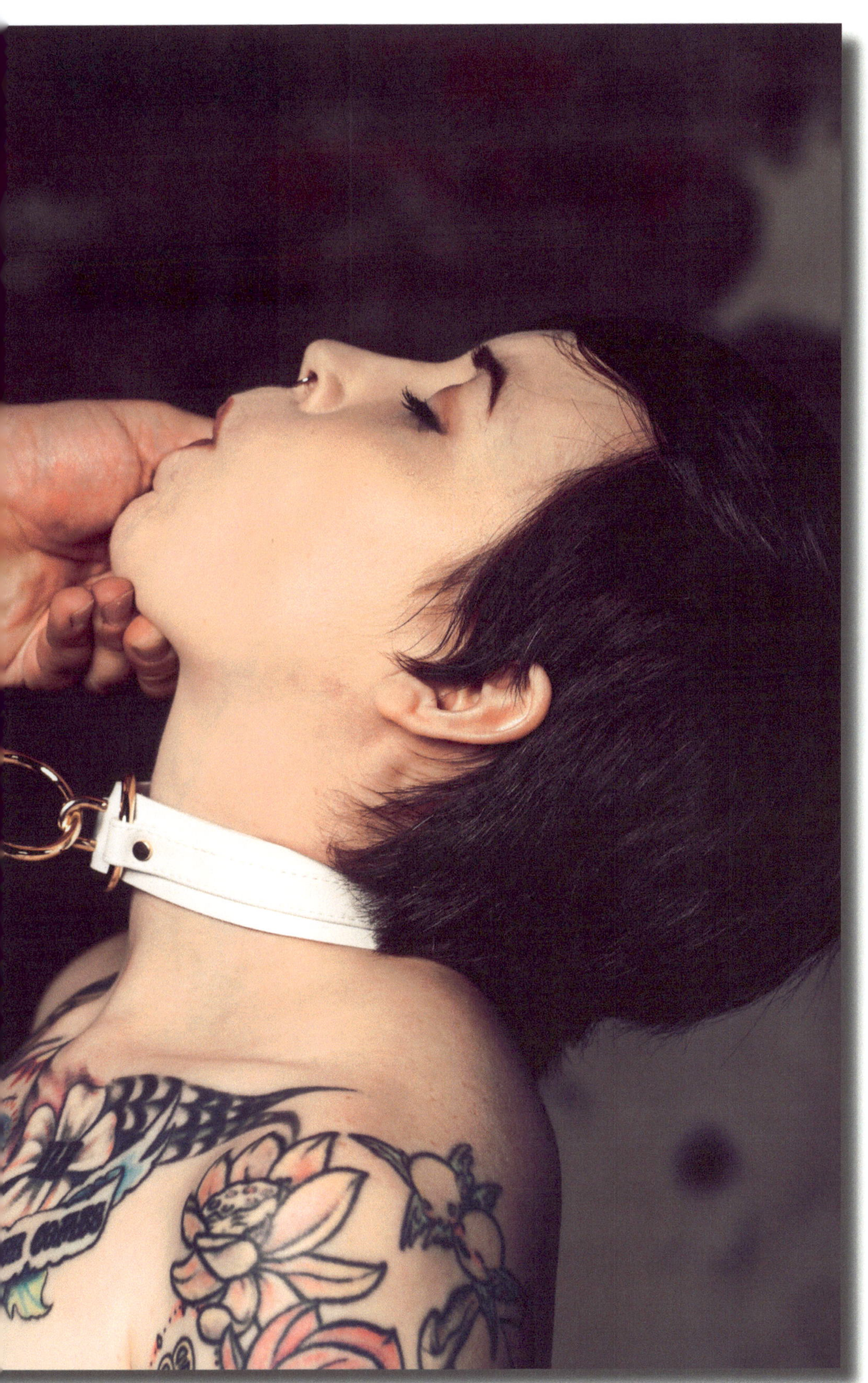

Yes, she was
a woman of class.
But when I grabbed
her throat,
when I tied her down,
when I spanked
and whipped her,
oh boy.
Who could have guessed
how filthy
her soul could become.
How ready she was
to let go of everything.
How much she craved for
my dirty, shameless sins.

The more you try to
run away from me,
the more scared you are
of the filthy pleasures
I give to your body and mind,
the more you will
find yourself on my doorstep.
On your knees,
begging me
to hurt you,
to hurt your soul.

57 Demons

A gentleman always carries two essential accessories;
a belt and tie.
You never know when you're going to need to
punish her,
tie her up or
shut her up

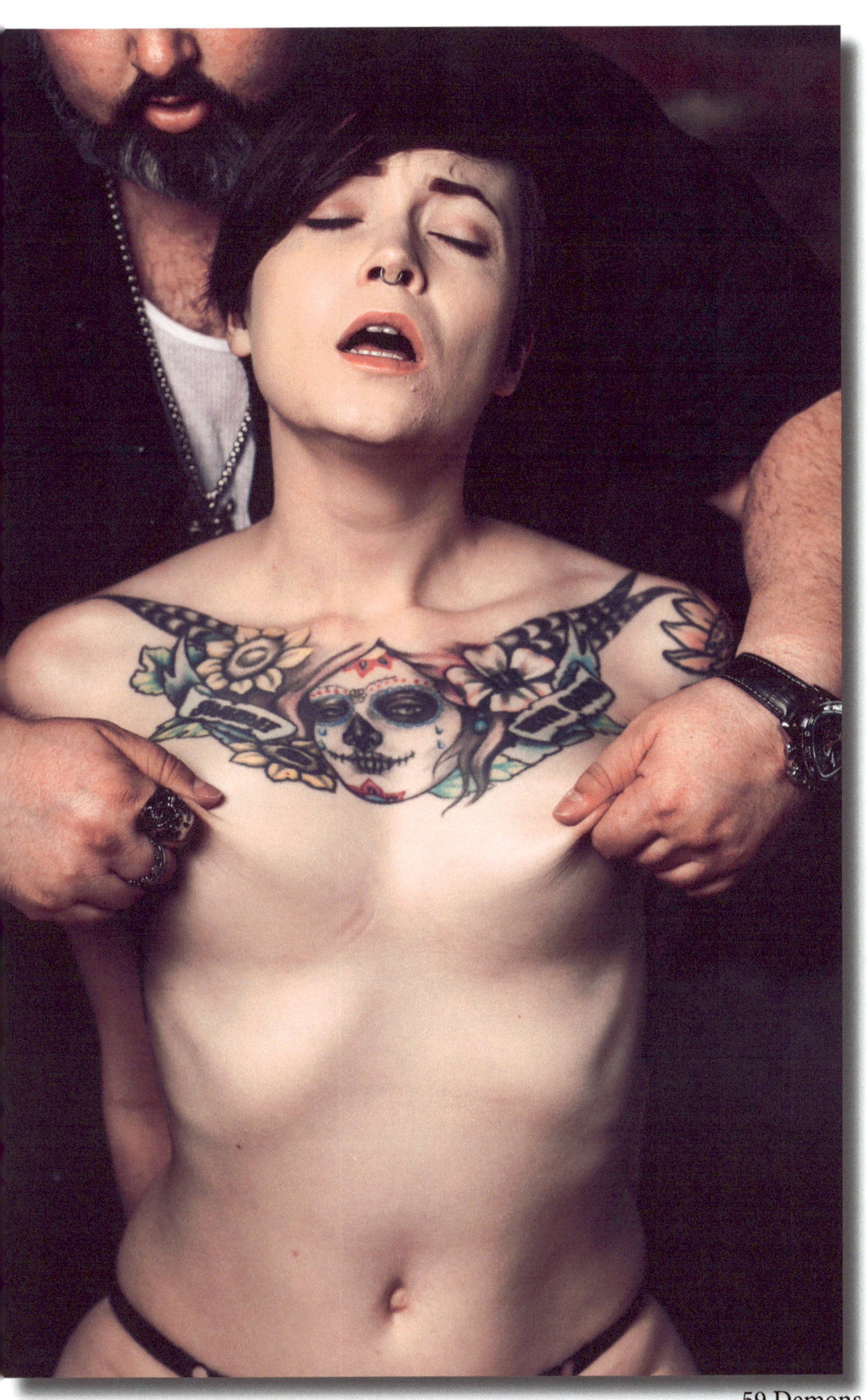

For the kiss that burns,
for the touch that wakes,
for the thrust that shakes,
for the spank that lingers;
You will spend a lifetime
trying to forget how they make you
throb and so wet between those lips.

Come here,
babygirl.
I will
give you
a pain
to erase
all the
pain
life has
given you
before me.

63 Demons

I always wondered
what heaven would
smell like,
until I kissed my way towards
your pussy with deep kisses
on your inner thighs.
Your scent that's mixed with
pleasure, adrenaline, and anticipation,
made me light headed.
I took a deep breath and
let it make me drunk.
I was in heaven when I
pressed my wide open mouth
against your soaked pussy
and pushed my tongue between
those throbbing sweet lips.

I will pin you down.
Whether I am fucking, kissing, rubbing,
licking, eating or fingering you.
I will make you feel that helplessness,
I will make you feel owned.
All which will make you soaking wet,
just the way I like my babygirl to be.

67 Demons

I will make you cum,
over and over again.
On the borderline of
pain and pleasure,
I will make you scream
while your body is bound
by the fabric of reality.
I will give you a dream
you will never want to wake up from.

I grabbed you from behind, suddenly.
Pulled you to myself so hard
as I pressed my body against yours.
My chest against your back.
My growing thickness
pressing between your cheeks.
My right hand grabbed your throat
as the left hooked your pussy harshly,
no gentleness to be found.
You let a loud gasp out
and lost the air from your lungs.
I whispered into your ear,
"You forgot who the fuck owns you."
I squeezed your body in my arms
with all my strength and lifted you up.
Your mind went crazy
as your body lifted off the floor.
You felt me taking all your control.
I turned around and faced the wall,
carrying you up in the air.
I slammed you against the wall,
pressing my body against you,
crushing you between me and the concrete.
"I told you, little princess,
whenever I want, wherever I want
and however I want."

Your most sinful moment
was not when I exploded inside you.
It was not when you swallowed every drop.
It was when you craved for me the next day.
It was when you could not stop thinking
how you felt at the moment my thick shaft
entered you for the first time.
It was when your whole body shivered
with the thought of my tongue
sliding between your wet lips.
It was when I called you the next day
and your pussy got wet instantly
when I said "Hi, babygirl."

This is a raw passion,
free from games and
free from illusions.
We are two freight trains
on a collision course,
head on at full speed.
We know there is no escape.
I know you can't even breathe.
You know I can't stay sane
without our skins touching,
so we give in to the lust.
Devouring each other again and again,
again and again with no rest.
A barbarous, monstrous fuck.
Hair pulling, throat grabbing,
ass spanking, pussy slapping,
nipple biting, clit sucking,
deepthroat, cumshot, creampie.
We consume every single term in
the urban dictionary that contains fucking.
I can`t get enough of hearing
you screaming, "Harder Daddy."
You get fiercer as I growl.
We can`t stop, wanting more and more.

If you misbehave,
I will hurt you.
If you misbehave again,
I will hurt you.
If you misbehave again,
I will hurt you again.
One day,
you will find
yourself misbehaving
because you are
craving so badly
for me to hurt you.

My soul has sinned.
My mind has sinned.
My body has sinned,
because
I fucking love
to drown in sin.
I love to bathe in sin.
I will thrust my sins
deep down into your throat,
until my creamy sins
stream down your lips.
Until you swallow
every drop of my sins.
My fucking little whore,
you will please all my sins
and you will cum screaming
for your Master,
as you consume all my sins
and look at me
with gorgeous sinful eyes.

You know what I love to do most?
I love to take that good girl,
that sweet girl who everybody knows
and use her for my pleasure.
Turn her into the little fucking whore
that I know very well.
I love to take
her body to her limits
and watch her scream with pleasure.
Watch her cum all over my thick cock
and be proud of what she becomes.
For me,
for her Master.

81 Demons

I know how thirsty
you are, my babygirl.
I saw it in your eyes
when I grabbed your hair
and made you kneel before me.
I saw your dry soul.
I saw your dry lips,
eagerly opened dry lips.
That worshipping look
in your eyes.
You've been thirsty
and craving for so long.
I am your fountain
that has been waiting for your lips.
It felt like an eternity,
but now you are here.
Open wide and take me in.
Make me moan, make me growl
and drink from your fountain
as my rivers of cream
run down your throat.

The more I give in
to the monster inside me
and feed him,
the more I get scared.
But oh God, I love it
to my bones.

I don`t give a fuck
who you are or were.
When I close the door
you belong to me.
You are my fucktoy.
You are my little whore,
and you will leave here
leaning against the walls.

87 Demons

I locked all your demons
down in the basement.
I reached down into your
darkest desires and fantasies.
I grabbed each and every one
of them by their throats.
I will own you here, babygirl.
They will listen to those
screams of yours
and tremble
when I tie them down, shaking.
They will get wet from your screams.
Once I`m finished with you
and leave you
as a sticky, hot mess on the floor,
I will bring your demons up
one by one
and fuck them
in front of your hungry eyes.

Some people
are more
comfortable
in hell,
that's why
I crawled
in between your legs.

She moaned,
louder and louder
as she started to cum.
Her body rocking,
her legs trembling,
she screamed, "Ohh my God!"
I whispered in her ear,
"You will scream
only my name, babygirl.
God doesn`t come where I go."

Curiosity
is a maddening thing my sweet babygirl,
is it not?
I`m curious how you will look up at me
when you get down on your knees.
I`m curious how your eyes
will burst into flames
when I thrust myself into you.
I`m curious how loud
you will scream when you cum
for your Master.
I`m curious how much
your voice will tremble
when the only thing
you can say is, "Yes Sir."

We people are the creature of habits.
My habit is to fuck you,
Kiss you;
Hug you;
Lick you;
Spank you;
Choke you;
Violate you;
Use you;
Please you;
Own you;
Tease you;
Whip you;
Tie you;
Cuff you;
Spank you,
over and over and over again.

Hope is the pump
that holds up the world
Hope is the dream
of a waking man.

I am the Leo.
I am the King.
I will roar and growl.
I will use you as I please.
Your scent will unleash me.
My teeth will make you scream.
My tongue will make you
tumble down the rabbit hole.
My belt will make you beg
for more and more and more.
But, in the end,
after my thickness has consumed
your mind and your soul,
you will be in my big arms;
safe, sound and still shaking.

99 Demons

I don`t want you.
I want your darkest side,
I want that frisky evil
you are hiding inside your soul.
Hiding from society,
hiding from your boyfriend and
hiding from your husband.
I am going to grab her horns
and push my thick,
rock hard shaft
between her begging lips.
Making her eyes burst into
flames with lust.
We will both burn to ashes
to be reborn in the lake of pleasure.

I don`t care which face
you show to everyone else.
Show them your cute face,
show them the girl next door face.
I know your sinful face.
I know your face
when I thrust my cock into you.
I know your face
when I eat your pussy.
I know your face
when you scream as you cum.
I know your face
when you submit yourself to me
on your knees.

103 Demons

I am a dreamer
chasing after dreams.
My desires are
fueled by my cravings,
my hunger and
my thirst.
Yet, being a dreamer
comes with a huge price.
Constant pain that lies
underneath the skin.
Waiting for a chance
to come out and remind me
that I am a fool
who keeps dreaming of things
I will never touch or kiss.
I am chained
to real life,
trying to reach my dreams.
I can almost touch them
with my fingertips.
I am yanking my chains,
cold iron cuts my skin
not letting me move.
Just one more inch,
I scream and yank again.
My tears and my blood
stain the dirty floor.
I scream and yank again,
my fingertips almost touching my dreams.
Just one more fucking inch.

Do you know why I love to
fuck your mind with my words first?
Why I like to invade
every corner of your soul
buried in darkness
before I even touch your flesh?
Before I thrust my hardness
into your soaked, throbbing lips?
Before I grab your throat
and look deep into your eyes?
When I own you with my words,
I can control you wherever you are.
You are mine
even when you are
on the other side of the planet.
I don`t have to physically touch you
to make you feel my power.
I am with you all the time.

I know you love
the gentleman in me
who writes poems for you.
Who send flowers to you
and who makes you laugh.
But, I also know you crave
for the beast in my shadows.
Who grabs your hair
and whispers into your ear.
Who owns your body
and your mind,
who grabs your throat
and squeezes the fucking brat
out of your smart mouth
while you moan and get so wet.
You crave for the beast
who dominates you
and takes you to the edge
of your limits.
You crave for the beast
who thrusts into you so deep,
over and over and over again.
Look deep into my eyes, babygirl,
you are about to unleash the beast.

I am going to own you.
I am going to punish you.
I am going to make you scream.
I am going to break you
into millions of pieces
as you cum for your Master,
over and over again.
Then, I am going to put you
back together.
You will love the new you
as I seal each piece
with my kisses.

I want you to be my last supper.
Laying on the table breathless,
legs wide open.
Your pussy dripping.
Your juice streaming down
from the edge of your lips
between your ass cheeks
to the table, creating a small puddle.
I want to eat your throbbing pussy
as my appetizer.
To make you scream loud
so the heavens above the clouds and
dungeons below hell are awakened.
I will climb on to the table,
devour your body and your soul
in a bowl mixed with our sins.
As my thick shaft destroys
your demons, hiding in the darkest
corners of your soul.
Those fucking demons
will disappear one by one
as you scream louder
and louder with each orgasm.
You will take my swollen shaft
as your dessert, deep down your throat.
It will still be spasming violently
while you suck and lick it clean.
I will not care if I go to
the seventh floor of hell.
I will not care, after my last supper.
I will not care, when my last heartbeat
is your eyes kissing my soul free.

Special thanks to

Model name	Pages appeared
Vivian Beck	6-7-21-31-34-35-37-41-45-48-49-51-55-57-61-75-79-81-83-87-95-97-99-103-107-109-110-111
Sorcery	2-4-25-39-43-52-53-59-65-67-69-71-73-85-89-90-91-92-93-101-105
Mandi Kramer	47-113-Back cover
Melissa Jean	9-11-13-15-17-18-19-22-23-28-29-33-62-63-77

Accesories used	Pages appeared
Premium Garment Leather Locking Waist Cuff by The Stockroom	90-91
www.stockroom.com	
Kinklab Leather Hog Tie Kit by The Stockroom	113
www.stockroom.com	

OWNED